I Love to Sing

For my brother "Fred"

SIMON & SCHUSTER BOOKS FOR YOUNG READERS
An imprint of Simon & Schuster Children's Publishing Division
1230 Avenue of the Americas, New York, New York 10020
Copyright © 2008 by Anna Walker
First published by Scholastic Australia Pty Limited in 2008
This edition published under license from Scholastic Australia Pty Limited
First U.S. edition 2011
All rights reserved, including the right of reproduction in whole or in part in any form.
SIMON & SCHUSTER BOOKS FOR YOUNG READERS is a trademark of Simon & Schuster, Inc.
For information about special discounts for bulk purchases, please contact
Simon & Schuster Special Sales at 1-866-506-1949 or business@simonandschuster.com.
The Simon & Schuster Speakers Bureau can bring authors to your live event.
For more information or to book an event, contact the Simon & Schuster
Speakers Bureau at 1-866-248-3049 or visit our website at www.simonspeakers.com.
The text for this book is handwritten by Anna Walker.
The illustrations for this book are rendered in ink on watercolor paper.
Manufactured in Singapore / 1110 TIW
10 9 8 7 6 5 4 3 2 1
Library of Congress Cataloging-in-Publication Data
Walker, Anna.
I love to sing / Anna Walker.—1st U.S. ed.
p. cm.
Summary: A zebra named Ollie celebrates the joys of singing in the bathtub,
with his dog, Fred, and in the park.
ISBN 978-1-4169-8322-4 (hardcover)
[1. Stories in rhyme. 2. Singing—Fiction. 3. Zebras—Fiction.] I. Title.
PZ8.3.W149Ial 2011
[E]—dc22
2010018986

I Love to Sing

by Anna Walker

SIMON & SCHUSTER BOOKS FOR YOUNG READERS

New York • London • Toronto • Sydney

My name is Ollie.

I love to sing.

I love to sing
on my chair.

I love to sing
on my stair.

I love to sing in the rain

and the sun,

and with my brother,
just for fun.

I love to sing with ducks

in the park.

Quack

I sing with Fred,

who loves to bark !

I love to sing

in the lemon tree

and in my bath
with a cup of tea.

But what I love best
is to sing in bed —
a happy song
for me and Fred!

More I Love Ollie books

I Love Christmas

I Love My Mom

I Love My Dad

I Love Vacations

I Love Birthdays

I Love to Dance